D1397619

A catalogue record for this book is available from the British Library

Published by Ladybird Books Ltd
A subsidiary of the Penguin Group
A Pearson Company

LADYBIRD and the device of a Ladybird are trademarks of
Ladybird Books Ltd Loughborough Leicestershire UK

First published by Ladybird Books Ltd MCMXCVI. This edition MCMXCVII

Text © Joan Stimson MCMXCV
Illustrations © Ladybird Ltd MCMXCV

The author/artist have asserted their moral rights

Telephone
~ TED ~

by Joan Stimson
illustrated by Peter Stevenson

Ladybird

The Teddy at Number Ten was bored.
His owner had just started school.
And Ted had too much time on his paws.

Brring, brring. Ted waited for Charlie's
mum to answer the phone. But the
washing machine was going flat out.
And she couldn't hear it.

Brring, brring...
Ted peeked round
the door.

Brring, brring...
he clambered
onto a chair.

And then...
brring, brring...
Ted picked up
the receiver!

"It's only me," said a cheerful voice. "I'd like to pop round after school and bring a cake."

Ted listened eagerly. Then he took a deep breath:

"Hi there, Grandma, that sounds great,
But what a shame I'll have to wait.
Is it chocolate? Is it coffee?
I LOVED the one with lumps of toffee."

But all Grandma heard was a grumbly growl. So she decided to ring back later.

The next day, as soon as
Mum left with Charlie,
the phone rang again.

Brring, brring...
Ted waited for a
few seconds.

Brring, brring...
then he picked it up.

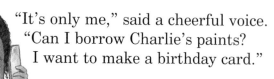

"It's only me," said a cheerful voice.
"Can I borrow Charlie's paints?
I want to make a birthday card."

Ted listened eagerly. Then he
took a deep breath:

"*WOW! Brenda, painting's fun,*
Especially when the colours run.
Come round tonight and
  don't forget.
We'll ALL try out
  the painting set."

But all Brenda heard was
a grumbly growl. So she
decided to ring back later.

One morning, Mum put up a new shelf.
Wheeee, whirr, whirr, wheeee! went the
electric drill.

Brring, brring… went the phone. And this
time Ted picked it up straightaway.

"It's only me," said a cheerful voice. "Your motorbike has been repaired, and is ready for collection."

"Brrmm! Brrmm!" replied Ted eagerly. Then he took a deep breath:

"I bet it goes just like a rocket,
I'd love to ride in someone's pocket.
I've never tried a motorbike,
But I'm an ace on Charlie's trike."

But all the mechanic heard was a grumbly growl. So he decided to ring back later.

By now Ted was fed up. "I wish I could have a PROPER telephone conversation!" he sighed.

Brring, brring... it was well into the afternoon.

Brring, brring... Charlie wasn't home from school.

Brring, brring...
and Mum had
gone out in her
best skirt.

Brring, brring...
"Oh, go away,"
growled Ted.

Brring, brring...
"You won't
understand a word
I say," he grumbled.

Brring, brring, brring, brring... on and on the phone rang.

Until, in the end, Ted snatched it up. And this time he spoke first:

> *"I've had a really rotten day,*
> *THEY'RE ALL OUT, so I can't play.*
> *I need a chat, I'm all alone,*
> *But no one LISTENS on the phone."*

But someone WAS listening.
In fact, the caller heard every single word!

The caller took a
deep breath and
then he replied:

"I'm Brenda's bear from Number Three,
If you stretch up, then you can see,
I'm waving on the window ledge.
It's brilliant now they've cut the hedge."

"I've got some news, it's really great!
I had to tell, I couldn't wait.
Charlie's been here, did you know?
Sorry, Ted, I've got to go..."

Ted looked across the street in amazement.
He could just see Brenda's bear in the window.
Then Charlie and Mum came hurrying home.

"I can't wait to tell Grandma," cried Mum. And
she dived for the phone. As soon as Grandma
answered, Mum squealed with excitement:

"I got it! I got it! I got the lovely hospital job."

"Oh, NO!" groaned Ted.
"Now I'll be on my own
EVEN MORE!"

But Ted was wrong.

Because, when Mum went to work, Brenda's mum became Charlie's childminder. She became Ted's bearcarer too! And Ted began to spend his days with Brenda's bear.

Somehow the two friends never ran out of conversation. And, if ever they missed each other when Ted went home... *brring, brring...*

THERE WAS ALWAYS THE PHONE!